# PINDULI

Houghton Mifflin Harcourt
Boston  New York

# PINDULI

## JANELL CANNON

The sun was low in the East African sky. The animals had been sleeping all through the hot afternoon, and now they began to stir.

Pinduli awoke before Mama Hyena, eager to explore.

"Don't go far," Mama yawned. "We must hunt soon. There has been so little to eat lately that we'll need all night to find enough to fill our bellies."

Pinduli promised to stay close and trotted away.

As Pinduli passed the water hole, she spied sleepy animals in the brush. She sniffed the air, which was rich with exquisite and mysterious smells. But something was not so exquisite—or mysterious. It was the smell of dog.

Pinduli's sharp ears picked up the soft pounding of pads on the dirt. She spotted a pack of wild dogs at play on a faraway ridge. And then they saw her.

The leader dashed toward Pinduli. The others trailed behind and yelped, "Watch out, Dog—it's a hyena!"

"Just a shrimpy one," Dog scoffed, coming closer. "If it didn't have all that stripy fur, those ears would make me think it was a baby elephant!"

The pack erupted into wheezing laughter and galumphed away, tongues lolling.

Pinduli had never given a thought to her ears. Were they really so big? She let them fall flat against her head. *Plip, plop.*

*I can hardly hear now,* Pinduli thought, but she kept her ears down.

"Ahem!" A rumbling voice came from the scrub. *"Ahem!"*

Pinduli whirled around. A lion! The little hyena poofed her mane and suddenly looked twice her size. She was sure that she was mighty fierce, but Lion just calmly looked her up and down. Then he leaned his old, scarred face nearer and said, "That prickly fringe hardly becomes you, young lady."

Pinduli's mane flopped as she hurried away. She had never given a thought to her coat. Was it really so straggly?

Pinduli circled back to the water hole, waded into the pool, and let the water soak into her fur. She figured that when the water ran off, her coat would lie flat. No more prickly fringe!

Zebra and two friends strolled over, their brown eyes glinting at the sight of the soggy little hyena. Pinduli didn't like their amused look. She tried to lower herself deeper into the water and disappear, but she was too late.

"If you're going to do stripes, please, please, please work on your symmetry and clarity! Good grooming—*not* soaking—will take some of that unpleasant haziness out of your patterns," whinnied Zebra. Then the three tossed their heads, dipped their lips into the water, and drank.

Pinduli splashed past the startled zebras and escaped to a quiet spot. Were her stripes really so disorderly? Didn't Mama Hyena always say she was the most beautiful hyena ever? She rolled and rolled in the pale dust, which stuck to her wet fur. Soon her soft stripes had completely vanished.

Ears pinned, coat flattened and dusted to a pallid gray, Pinduli wanted nothing more than to get home, hoping no one would notice her.

*I'm really in trouble now,* she worried. *I've been gone a long time, and Mama gets awful cranky when she's hungry.*

As she headed back to the rocky den, she saw Lion, Zebra, and Dog—along with his rowdy pals—hanging around the water hole. A few wildebeests were there, too, for an evening drink.

*My, it's busy out here tonight,* thought Pinduli, edging away from the others. No luck—the animals turned to see who was coming.

Their jaws dropped. Their eyes bulged. Pinduli looked around wildly. What did they see?

"A GHOST!" the animals screamed. "An evil spirit is upon us!"
They jumped and ran.

"Where? Where?!" cried Pinduli as she raced behind them.
Feet pounded and dust flew, and no one answered.

The terrified crowd tore through thorny brush, over craggy stone—and, horrified, found themselves at a dead end in a small canyon. They screeched to a halt, huddling closely, as they turned to face their worst fear.

Dog was the first to speak. "O Great Spirit!" he howled. "You've come for me—I know it! Because I made fun of a young hyena's ears."

All eyes were on Pinduli. *Ah. So I'm the ghost,* she thought. *I'd better get in character before they recognize me.*

"Go on, Dog," said Pinduli, in a slow, deep voice. "The Spirits want to know why you would commit such a hideous, awful, atrocious crime."

Dog's voice quavered. "I—I don't know. I guess I was still mad at Fennec Fox for calling me Butterfly Head."

Lion joined in. "Please spare us your wrath! I, too, have spread discord, by insulting a young hyena's mane. But Vulture called my own mane a mange!"

Pinduli nodded sagely.

Zebra stomped her hoof. "Owl told me that my stripes were garish." A tear rolled down her long face.

Everyone fell silent. Pinduli's mind whirled as she tried to think of what a ghostly spirit might say.

*Of course! Spirits always give tasks and want offerings!* she thought. *Hmmm…let's see…okay—Mama will love this!*

"In order to appease bad spirits, you must find your tormentors and make peace," Pinduli called out with authority. "And always leave a bit of every meal as an offering. If you do this, I shall never return." She turned and glided away on her tiptoes, trying not to smile.

"Thank you! Thank you!" called the creatures. "We will do as you say."

Once out of sight, Pinduli raced home.

"There you are!" cried Mama Hyena as Pinduli galloped up to her. "You look awful!"

Pinduli was so glad to be home again, it was worth getting in trouble. She didn't even mind the five baths it took to get the dirt out of her fur. In fact, it took all night to get Pinduli looking like a beautiful hyena again.

"I was worried sick—I went looking everywhere for you!" said Mama Hyena as she helped smooth Pinduli's coat. "Now that you're all straightened up, we've got to get out and find something to eat. It's already morning, and I'm sure you are as ravenous as I am."

Pinduli's stomach growled.

That very morning, Dog, Lion, and Zebra searched the wide savanna until they found Fennec Fox, Vulture, and Owl.

"We have come here on the order of the Great Spirit," Dog announced. "We must find out why you were so rude to us."

Fennec Fox spoke up. "I guess I was having a bad day. Serval Cat said I looked like a little fuzzy bat without wings." He nodded to Dog. "Your ears really aren't so bad."

Vulture ducked his bald head. "Marabou Stork called me Moonscape…So I got mad and made fun of Lion."

Owl moaned, "Adder said my feathery stripes look more like scribbles."

"Let's go find those three and get to the bottom of this," said Dog.

The oddball crowd went searching and found Serval, Marabou, and Adder.

"We've come here on the order of the Great Spirit," they declared.

"Uh-oh. I'm in trouble for laughing at Owl's stripes," hissed Adder. "Miss Zebra, do you remember…"

"…when I said your stripes were dull?" mumbled Zebra.

Marabou stepped forward on his stilt-like legs. "Lion told me that the glare of the sun on my head hurt his eyes."

"Sorry," grumbled the big, bald cat.

Then Dog blurted, "Oh, dear. Serval, please forgive me."

Serval's amber eyes squinted at Dog. "You mean for the time you said that the wind might pick me up by my giant ears and blow me away?" he said.

"Yep," Dog yipped. "Who am I to be talking about ears?" He pranced about, flopping his big ears like the wings of a butterfly. Serval burst out laughing—and everyone, including Dog, joined in.

From that day on, things began to change for Pinduli and her mother. Instead of spending hours hungrily scrounging for meager meals, they found delicious treats everywhere.

"Look—again! Eggs! Fish! Fruit! It's a miracle!" exclaimed Mama.

As Pinduli tasted a sweet berry, she said, "The Great Spirit must be smiling upon us!"

Mama Hyena looked at her grinning daughter. "Wait a minute—did you have something to do with this?"

Laughing and feasting, Pinduli told the whole story.

"You're not only the most beautiful hyena ever," said Mama, "you're the smartest hyena ever!"

# MEET THE HYENA FAMILY

All hyenas look like dogs in many ways, but actually they are a unique family of their own, called the Hyaenidae. Within this family, there are four species.

The striped hyena (*Hyaena hyaena*) is less well known than other hyenas because of its nocturnal habits, solitary hunting, small clans, and a tendency to live in inhospitable places. Its habitat ranges from eastern and northern Africa to areas of the Middle East, Asia, and India. Its coat of long fur can be yellow to light gray, with black vertical stripes, and it has a mane along its back. When startled, the striped hyena can raise the mane to make itself look bigger

and more intimidating. These animals can grow to be more than a hundred pounds, and they eat just about anything—from bugs to fruit to small animals.

Conflicting reports describe them as both timid and bold. Perhaps, like people, each hyena has its own personality.

The spotted hyena (*Crocuta crocuta*) is well known and often is called the "laughing hyena." The famous "laugh" is a sound it makes when agitated or excited. None of the other hyena species makes this unique call. With its colorful vocabulary of whoops, growls, and cackles, it belongs to the loudest and rowdiest branch of the hyena family. It is also the largest of the four species—growing up to 150 or so pounds—and it is very social. Often, up to eighty of them will run together in a group called a clan. The females are larger than the males and lead the clans. Spotted hyenas range throughout most of Africa, except in the deepest jungles and driest deserts. They are very good hunters, and with their powerful jaws, the hyenas can rapidly consume any large prey, bones and all.

The brown hyena (*Parahyaena brunnea*) lives only in the southern tip of Africa. It is about the same size as the striped hyena, and, like its striped cousin, it hunts on its own but stays close to a small clan of family members. It eats a wide variety of foods, from carrion, insects, and small animals to eggs, vegetables, and fruit.

The aardwolf (*Proteles cristatus*) is the smallest member of the hyena family, rarely reaching a weight of more than thirty pounds. *Aardwolf*, a word in the Afrikaans language, means "earth wolf," apparently referring to the aardwolf's tendency to live in underground burrows.

Aardwolves live in eastern Africa and southern Africa. They are believed to be the only members of the hyena family that don't live in clans. The aardwolf lacks the great bone-crushing jaws of the bigger hyenas and has more delicate teeth, better suited to crunching bugs. Its diet consists mostly of insects, and termites are the aardwolf's favorite food. Instead of breaking into termite nests, the aardwolf finds termites on the ground at night and simply laps them up with its tongue.

# WHY ARE SOME ANIMALS BALD?

The marabou stork and the vulture are meat-eating scavengers. To get enough to eat during the typically vigorous competition for a carcass, they move quickly and aggressively, which makes for a messy meal.

After eating, the bird will groom its feathers. It can reach every part of its body but its head. If these birds had feathery heads, they'd have a terrible time trying to clean their matted plumage. Being bald helps them stay clean and healthy.

A bald male African lion? They do exist, especially in the Tsavo area of Kenya, where they are being studied by scientists. Although male lions in Tsavo do have fur on their heads, they don't have long, shaggy manes. Tsavo is a dry, hot place, thick with prickly brush that easily tangles with long fur. Perhaps these lions have adapted to the conditions by shedding their manes. Being less bulky and conspicuous also may allow the male lions to be stealthier hunters.

Throughout Africa, male lions sport a wide variety of manes—color can range from golden blond to dark brown. Some have thin, short manes and receding hairlines; others have long, shaggy mop tops.

## WHY ARE OTHERS STRIPED?

Many wonder why zebras have
such a bold black-and-white display.
Some say that when a herd of zebras
is disturbed by a predator, the wild
pattern of stripes creates a "dazzle effect"
that confuses their pursuers. Others
guess that the zebra's stripes provide
unusual air-conditioning in the sweltering
climate where it lives. The black stripes
draw in the hot sunlight, while the white
stripes reflect it—creating cooling air
currents around the zebra's whole body.
It's possible that the variations between
the stripes of different zebras are a way for
them to attract and identify each other.

The African eagle owl
and the adder are predators,
and they use their stripes to
hide themselves when they
hunt. The stripes also help
these creatures to stay hidden
from other predators. The
owl's feather stripes mimic the patterns of
tree bark, while the adder's stripes blend
with leaves and rocks
on the ground.

## AND WHY THE BIG EARS?

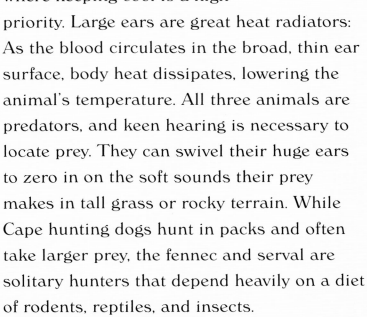

The Cape hunting dog,
fennec fox, and serval have
big ears in common. They
all live in hot, dry climates,
where keeping cool is a high
priority. Large ears are great heat radiators:
As the blood circulates in the broad, thin ear
surface, body heat dissipates, lowering the
animal's temperature. All three animals are
predators, and keen hearing is necessary to
locate prey. They can swivel their huge ears
to zero in on the soft sounds their prey
makes in tall grass or rocky terrain. While
Cape hunting dogs hunt in packs and often
take larger prey, the fennec and serval are
solitary hunters that depend heavily on a diet
of rodents, reptiles, and insects.

For Alice J. Contreras

The illustrations in this book were done in Liquitex acrylic
and Prismacolor pencils on Bristol board.
The display lettering was created by Judythe Sieck.
The text type was set in Windsor Light.

The Library of Congress has cataloged the hardcover edition as follows:
Cannon, Janell, 1957–
Pinduli/Janell Cannon.
p. cm.
Cannon/PINDULI
Summary: Pinduli, a young striped hyena, is hurt by the unkind words of Dog, Lion, and Zebra,
but her clever trick in return promotes her clan's survival and spreads harmony throughout the savanna.
Includes back matter notes about hyenas and other animals of the African savanna.
[1. Kindness—Fiction. 2. Individuality—Fiction. 3. Tricksters—Fiction.
4. Hyenas—Fiction. 5. Savanna animals—Fiction.] I. Title. PZ7.C1725Pi 2004 [E]—dc22 2003021297

ISBN: 978-0-15-204668-2 hardcover
ISBN: 978-1-328-74050-2 paperback

Manufactured in Italy
7
4500839981

ACKNOWLEDGMENTS

Thanks to Randell Herren, San Diego Zoo senior animal caretaker,
for first introducing me to the striped hyena, and Janet Hawes from the
San Diego Zoo nursery, who shared valuable anecdotes about raising hyena cubs.

Further thanks to Amy Roberts, head curator at the Desert Zoo in Palm Desert,
for introducing me to Cydney Hawes, who cares for Gregor and Kisa,
the only striped hyenas currently on exhibit in Southern California.

And more thanks to Nancy Rapp, who introduced me to the Saint Louis Zoo staff,
who in turn shared their knowledge and enthusiasm about spotted hyenas: Ron Goellner,
Mary Ann Weiss, Laura Seger, Carrie Osborne, and Carol Stephenson,
who can maneuver a zoo cart just about anywhere.

Finally, thanks to Aaron Wagner,
who is studying the mysterious striped hyena of Kenya, Africa.